FEATHERY FABLES

CONTENTS

D1044479

FEATHERY

Storytelling has been around nearly as long as spoken language. The earliest written stories date back four thousand years. But some people did not write down their stories. Instead, oral storytellers handed down stories from generation to generation. The storytellers were important people. Their stories were not only entertaining, they also taught about historical events, beliefs, and morals. Many of these stories have now been collected and written down so that people all around the world can enjoy them.

There are many different types of stories. The stories in this collection are *fables*. A fable is a short story that uses animals to teach a

FICTION

moral or lesson. The stories in *Feathery Fables* are about birds, either by themselves, as in "The Mother Bird," or in magical interactions with people, as in "The Snow Bird."

Birds are popular images in fiction. Perhaps this is because people have always been intrigued by birds' ability to fly. Or maybe it is simply because birds are found all around the world. Whatever the reason, birds appear not only in stories, but in songs, poems, and *proverbs*, or sayings, as well. We have included some "feathery" proverbs at the end of this collection. Perhaps you could think of some more "feathery" sayings, or even come up with some of your own.

New Mexico

THE MOTHER BIRD

*The lesson to be learned
from this Pueblo Indian story
from New Mexico is that it
pays to never give up.*

1 t was hot in New Mexico. Crow found shade in a tall tree, and there she built her nest and laid her eggs. She stretched her soft black wings and cradled them over the eggs.

"I will wait here until my babies hatch," she said.

So she sat and waited. The bright golden sun rose and set and rose and set again. Crow became impatient and bored.

"I'm sick of just sitting here waiting," she said.

She watched other birds soar through the sky past the treetops and over the hills.

"I don't think these eggs are ever going to hatch!" she said. And then she flapped her wings and flew off with the wind.

A little while later, Hawk was passing by. She saw Crow's eggs in the nest and waited for her to return. But Crow did not come back.

"I'd better keep the eggs warm," Hawk thought.

She stretched her wings and nestled gently on top of the eggs. She waited and waited. The sun set behind the hills. It peeped up over the horizon in the morning. And still Hawk waited.

"These eggs are taking a long time to hatch," she thought. "But I can't give up."

Finally, a tiny tapping sound came from inside the eggs. Slowly, Hawk helped the baby crows out of their speckled shells. She hunted for food and fed them. Days went by and the little crows began to grow.

One day, Crow flew past. She saw the small birds in the nest she had made.

"My eggs did hatch!" she said happily.

Then she saw Hawk returning with food.

"Hawk, what are you doing in my nest?" she asked angrily.

Hawk looked at Crow. "I'm feeding your chicks because you left!"

"Well, they're my chicks and I'm back now," Crow said. "So off you go!"

But Hawk wouldn't go. "You went away and left those eggs, so the chicks belong to me now!" she squawked.

"We'll see about that!" said Crow. "We shall ask Great Eagle. We shall see what he has to say about it!"

So Crow and Hawk flew to the nest of Great Eagle. He tilted his wise head to one side as he listened to their story.

There was silence as the wind fluttered his magnificent feathers.

Then he said, "We shall ask the little crows who they think their mother is."

So they flew back to Crow's nest. Eagle proudly led the way, and Crow and Hawk followed nervously behind.

"Who is your mother?" Eagle asked the little crows.

They looked at Hawk and chirped excitedly. "This is our mother!" they said.

Eagle turned to Crow, who was now crying and hanging her head in shame.

"I am sorry, little Crow, but you gave up and left. Hawk did not, and she was rewarded. Let this be a lesson."

Crow flew off feeling very sad. But she never gave up on anything ever again!

Western Samoa

The Magic Bird

*T*his tale is from Western
Samoa. It teaches that by helping
others we often help ourselves.

any years ago, on the island of Savaii in Western Samoa, there lived a great canoe builder. His son Lata would watch him work and say, "One day, I shall make canoes too!"

Sefo and Simi, the canoe builder's other sons, would play with their friends. But Lata always sat and watched his father create beautiful hulls from Tava tree logs.

One day, the father said to his sons, "It's time you each made a canoe."

Eagerly, the boys set off to choose their logs. Sefo reached the heart of the forest first and began clearing away the ferns. As he worked, he heard a small voice.

"Please help me!"

Sefo stopped and lifted his head to listen. There was a scuffling sound coming from the undergrowth. He peered through the ferns and saw a bird called a ve'a. A snake was coiled around its leg. The bird was beating its wings and bravely trying to fight off the snake.

"Please help!" it called again.

Sefo thought about helping the bird, but he was in a hurry.

"I haven't got enough time!" he said, and quickly set to work hacking at a tree trunk.

But, with every blow of his ax, not a single mark was made. It was as if the tree refused to be felled. Puzzled, Sefo shook his head, wiped the perspiration from his face, and angrily walked home.

Soon Simi came to the same spot.

"These trees are just right!" he thought.

As he got ready to start chopping, he heard a voice calling out for help.

When he saw the ve'a, he stopped in surprise. "What do you want me to do?"

"Free me from the snake!" cried the bird.

"I can't – it would take me too long to hack my way through all that bush!" said Simi, and he turned and started chopping at a tree.

But, with every chop, not a single mark was made. He stopped for a rest, panting and holding his side. Then he gave one almighty whack – but it was as if the ax had never touched the tree. So, in a great rage, Simi stomped home.

Then Lata came through the trees.

"Help me!" cried the bird.

When Lata saw the poor bird struggling with the snake, he immediately began hacking through the undergrowth.

"Don't worry, bird, I will help you!" he said, and soon the bird was free.

Gently, Lata scooped it up and stroked its trembling feathers. He cracked open a coconut and fed the bird its milk. Lata felt warm inside and was glad he had helped.

The bird looked into Lata's eyes. "Thank you. Your help will not be forgotten."

In a flash, the bird flew off. Lata began chopping down the tree and, suddenly, there in the dusk light, the tree turned into the most beautiful canoe Lata had ever seen!

Korea

The Brave Bird

T his story from Korea teaches
that acts of kindness often come back.

The gachi bird is the treasure bird of
Korea and is highly honored. If a
gachi sings in the morning on a
person's lawn, it is a good omen.

Once upon a time, there lived a Korean man named Kapsu. He had been traveling all day and was tired. As he walked through the forest, he heard a frightened bird calling for help.

He looked up in the trees and saw a treacherous green snake poised above a nest. A mother gachi bird was trying to defend her chicks. Kapsu had children of his own. In a flash, without thinking of his own danger, he scared away the snake with a stick. The gachi bird gave him a grateful look and then circled over him. Kapsu smiled and went on his way.

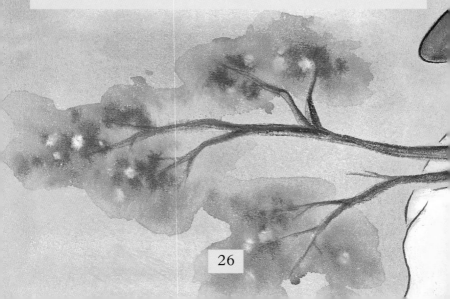

As the sun sank over the hill, Kapsu came to a village. He knocked on the door of a Jumak, a Korean inn, and asked Suhong, the owner, for a room.

Kapsu was shown to a room and soon fell fast asleep.

Early in the morning, he awoke to the sound of shouting downstairs. Then he heard footsteps in the hallway, and his door was thrown open.

"It is him!" said Suhong.

A guard seized Kapsu roughly.

"What is this about?" he asked.

"You stole from me!" cried Suhong. "It must have been you, because no one else slept here last night!"

"It wasn't me!" said Kapsu. "I have been asleep."

Kapsu shook his head in despair as he was taken through the streets and thrown into prison.

It was a custom in this village that prisoners were given seven days to prove their innocence. If they couldn't, they would be locked up forever. Sadly, Kapsu was a stranger and had no friends in the village who could vouch for his honesty.

When the sixth day approached, the guard spoke to him.

"There is a law here that if someone climbs the mountain to the temple and rings the bell three times, the prisoner is set free."

Kapsu hung his head. "No one would do that for me!" he sighed. Tears slid down his face and fell onto the earthen floor. "It is useless – I shall be locked up forever. I will never see my family again!"

The seventh day dawned. The sun peeped over the hill, and Kapsu's heart sank. Then, suddenly, as the sun rose high into the sky, there was a sound. It was the temple bell. The villagers shouted in the street.

"The bell is ringing!" they cried. "The prisoner shall go free!"

The guard unlocked the door. "You are free!" he said. "Somewhere you have a good friend!"

Kapsu was determined to find out who had saved him, so he climbed the high mountain. It took him all day, and the sweat glistened like crystals on his skin.

At the top was the temple. Kapsu paused before climbing the steep stairs to the bell. There, beside the bell, was the gachi bird he had helped. She was faint and weak with exhaustion from hitting the bell with her beak. Kapsu picked her up and held her close. He could feel her feeble heartbeat against his hand. Gratefully, he looked into her eyes.

"You have saved me, little one!" he said softly. "And you nearly died in doing so!"

He took the bird home and nursed her back to health. When she was better, Kapsu took her to the forest and set her free. But he knew that they would always be friends!

Japan

THE SNOW BIRD

*T*his story from Japan teaches
how important it is to keep promises.

*The Japanese regard the tancho
crane, or snow bird, as a symbol of
long life, peace, and happiness.*

35

Long, long ago, in the north of Japan, there lived a kindly old couple. They were very poor. All day, the man would cut wood and make it into charcoal to sell in the town. The woman would busy herself in the kitchen and dream of the children she had never had.

"If only I had just one daughter!" she would sigh as the steam rose from the pot.

One day, the old man was returning home from town. It was cold. An icy wind played with his hair and tugged at his trousers. Then, suddenly, he heard a cry. He stopped still. At his feet he saw a beautiful white-feathered crane caught in a trap. Red blood traced a pattern into the snow.

"You poor creature!" said the old man. "Just stay still, and I will help you out!"

The crane bent its graceful head and placed it on the man's shoulder. Soon the trap was open.

"There — fly free little one!" said the gentle old man.

The crane flapped its white wings and flew high into the winter sky. It circled the old man once and uttered a long, shrill cry. And then it was gone.

When the man returned home, he told his wife about the beautiful bird.

"You came along to help at just the right time!" said the old woman.

Much later, there was a knock on the door. The old man opened it and there stood a girl. Her hair was as black as the midnight sky, and she wore a kimono of white shimmering satin.

"Please help me," she said. "I'm lost."

"Come in," said the old man.

He gave her his place by the fire, the old woman made her a warm drink, and the girl stayed for the night.

The next day, there was a terrible storm.

"You cannot leave today," said the old man. "It is too cold outside."

"You can stay with us as long as you like," said the old woman.

The girl looked at the couple, and tears fell down her pale cheeks.

"I have nowhere to go. Could I stay here and be your daughter?" she asked.

"Of course you can!" said the couple at once. "It would make us very happy."

And so the season changed, the world became pink with cherry blossoms, and the old couple finally had a daughter.

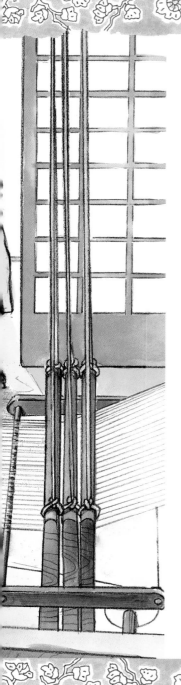

One day, the girl asked, "Could I please use the loom in the workroom?"

"Why, of course you can," said the old woman. "I haven't woven anything for many years."

The loom was thick with dust, but the old woman cleaned it and the girl sat down to begin weaving.

"I want you both to promise never to watch me while I work. Never, ever must you open this door!"

The old couple thought this was a very odd request, but they loved their new daughter, so they promised never to watch her at work.

The door stayed closed, and all day there was the sound of the clicking loom. The girl did not come out for her evening meal. The old couple waited up, but, finally, they went to bed. Their daughter continued to work throughout the night. The next morning, the door opened, and the girl stood holding the cloth she had woven. It was the most beautiful material the couple had ever seen.

"It's magnificent!" said the old man.

"Take it into town – it will bring you much more money than charcoal," the girl said.

Eagerly, the old man set off. When the townspeople saw the beautiful material, they were amazed.

"It is absolutely exquisite!" cried one woman.

"Show it to the lord of the castle!" said the crowd, and they took the old man up the castle steps.

The lord was very pleased with the beautiful material and immediately said, "I will buy it!" He gave the old man many gold coins. The man was just about to leave when the lord said, "Would you bring me some fine brocade for my daughter's wedding kimono?"

"I will try," said the old man, and he hurried home.

When the old man saw how pale and tired his daughter looked, he was almost afraid to ask for more cloth. So he thanked her, and shyly told her about the lord's wish.

"I can do it," she said. "But you must promise me again that you will never open the door while I am working."

The couple looked at each other.

"You must both promise or I cannot work!"

The couple nodded and promised solemnly.

So the girl began to work. The clicking of the loom continued through the day, into the darkness of night, and all the next day.

"She needs to rest!" said the old woman.

"But we must leave her be," said the man.

"I wonder why we cannot open the door? It is very strange."

The old man frowned.

"Why don't we have a little peep? Just to see if she's all right!" suggested the woman.

"But we promised not to!"

Finally, curiosity got the better of them. They couldn't resist it. They had to have a look. So, slowly and silently, the old woman pushed open the door.

To their surprise and shock, there at the loom sat a crane! It plucked a feather from its

thin body and wove it into the fabric. The old woman quickly closed the door.

"Our daughter is a crane!" she said. "How can this be?"

"She must be the crane I saved!" said the old man in astonishment.

The next morning, the door opened, and the girl, who was now very thin and tired looking, stood with her arms full of dazzling brocade.

"It is finished," she said. Then she looked into the old man's eyes. "But I cannot make any more cloth for you because you broke your promise. Yes, I am your crane daughter, but now I must leave you."

The girl lifted her thin arms, and they became soft feathered wings. Then, without a backward glance, she flew out the open window toward the rising sun.

And the old couple never saw their crane daughter again.

Feathery Proverbs

- Don't count your chickens before they hatch.

- The early bird catches the worm.

- A bird in the hand is worth two in the bush.

- Wise as an owl.

- Like water off a duck's back.

- One swallow does not a summer make.

- Birds of a feather flock together.

- What's good for the goose is good for the gander.

From the Author

I love stories. I like to read them and write them. I also love to tell them! The great thing about being a storyteller is that you can adapt your story to suit your audience.

My husband grew up in Savaii, Western Samoa – the setting for "The Magic Bird." He remembers the village storytellers telling stories to the children. He also remembers how the stories used to differ from storyteller to storyteller.

When the Korean story "The Brave Bird" was told to me, I was sad because the bird died. But because I was the storyteller in *Feathery Fables*, I was able to make my little gachi live!

Carol Krueger

That's a Laugh

Thrills and Spills

Challenges and Choices

Our Wild World

© Text by **Carol Krueger**
Illustrated by **Donna Humphries** (The Mother Bird); **George Taulealea** (The Magic Bird); **Meng-Feng Wu** (The Brave Bird); **Helen Humphries** (The Snow Bird)
Edited by **Frances Bacon**
Designed by **Nicola Evans**

04 03 02 01 00
10 9 8 7 6 5 4 3 2

Distributed in the United States by
   RIGBY
   a division of Reed Elsevier Inc.
   P.O. Box 797
   Crystal Lake, IL 60039-0797

Printed in Hong Kong.
ISBN: 0-7699-0429-7